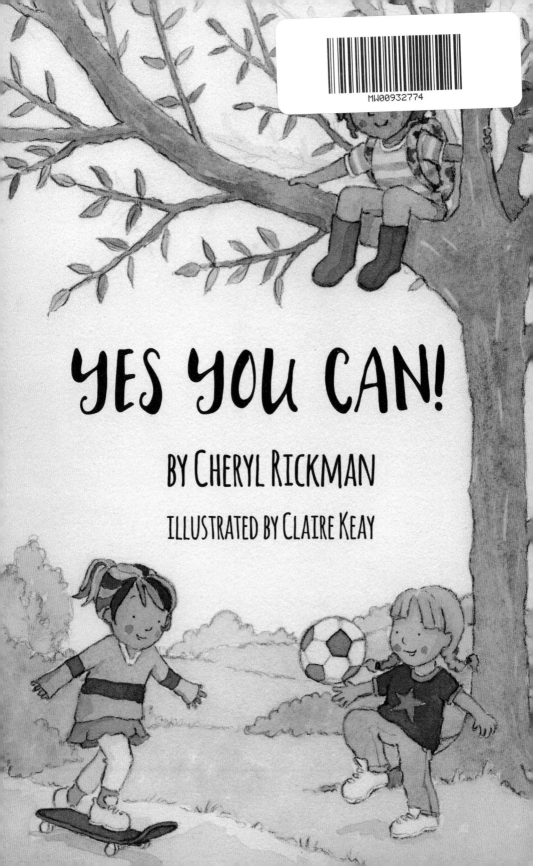

YES YOU CAN!

BY CHERYL RICKMAN

ILLUSTRATED BY CLAIRE KEAY

YES YOU CAN!

Illustrated by Claire Keay

ISBN-13: 978-1546806127
ISBN-10: 1546806121

For Brooke

YES YOU CAN!

BY CHERYL RICKMAN

ILLUSTRATED BY CLAIRE KEAY

The Climbing Trees Girls wouldn't have found the doorway to another world if it hadn't been for Maxi's grazed knee.

They'd been playing hide-n-seek, as they often did.

The three friends loved playing outdoors.

If Eva wasn't up a tree, she'd be in a woodland den. If she wasn't in a woodland den, she'd be fishing on the river.

Maxi, meanwhile, would always be found making something-or-other: making music, making a paper aeroplane, or painting a picture. If she wasn't creating, she'd be skateboarding.

B, on the other hand, loved football. She played it before school, at school and after school.

Each had big ideas about what they wanted to be when they grew up. Eva wanted to be a scientist, Maxi wanted to be a skateboarding artist and B wanted to be? Can you guess? …

A footballer of course!

And nothing was going to stop them.

That day, a cool breeze tickled the trees.

"Coming ready or not," giggled Maxi as she sped towards the sound of rustling leaves.

Eva had already clambered half-way up the old oak before Maxi and B rounded the corner.

Suddenly, Maxi tripped on a tree root. "Owwwww!" she howled.

Eva swung from a low branch to help her friend and landed just behind Maxi. But, when Maxi and B turned around to help her up, Eva wasn't there!

The two girls stepped towards the spot where Eva should have landed and whoosh!

They disappeared.

A sponge green carpet of moss gave B and Maxi a soft landing.

Eva stood nearby. She dusted herself off, looking as bewildered as they felt.

"Eva!" called B.

"Where are we?" asked a wide-eyed Maxi.

Eva shrugged.

A village stretched out in front of them, bustling with activity.

A man with a shiny bald head and a long red beard walked past them in a hurry. He didn't smile.

A child held her mum's hand and looked up at Eva, Maxi and B with big round eyes and smiled when she saw Maxi's skateboard.

"Mumma! Look! A skateboard!"

"Shush dear one," said her mummy. "You know that's not for you. You've got blonde hair and only people with red hair can play with skateboards."

The girls looked at each other and frowned as the no-longer-smiling child was whisked off into a toy shop.

Eva, Maxi and B followed.

To their surprise, all of the toys were separated with signs over each section indicating which toys were for which shade of hair colour.

"But, I don't like playing with dolls," said blond-haired B, reaching for a football.

At that moment, an alarm went off.

B shrunk back as a tall man with a wavy blonde-beard appeared from nowhere.

"You can't touch that," he said. "Only dark haired people are allowed sporty toys."

B raised her eyebrows at Maxi, who raised her eyebrows at Eva, and out of the shop they walked.

"No wonder everyone here seems miserable," they whispered.

A pair of red-haired twins walked past, their shoulders hunched and their faces blank. The girls decided to follow them to investigate further.

The twins, a girl and a boy, sloped off round a corner towards a skatepark.

Maxi's eyes lit up.

Skating was her spark. She loved the feeling she got when she landed on her board after a jump.

The twins, however, looked less pleased to be there. Still, they didn't have much choice, so they hired a skateboard from the kiosk and, like robots, stepped onto them and rode off, smile-less.

Maxi caught the girl's eye. "Don't you like skateboarding?" she asked with a friendly smile.

"No," whispered the girl as she zipped up her pink hoody. "But I can't let anyone know that or I'll be in trouble."

She could tell Maxi wasn't from the village because she seemed happy.

"What do you like?" asked B.

"I really love dolls and netball," said the girl. "And he likes dolls too," she smiled. "And Lego."

"We're not allowed to play with any of those things though," the boy added.

"Only blonde haired people get to play with dolls. Dark haired people get sports games and brown haired people get construction toys."

"We're only allowed to play with stuff on wheels," sniffed the girl.

"C'mon, we'd better go!" said the boy, and off they glumly skated.

After watching Maxi do some amazing moves, the girls stood and people-watched.

A girl with jet black curls ran past in trainers with a ball under her arm.

A brown-haired man in an orange jumper strolled past carrying a heavy-looking toolkit.

A blonde-haired mother scurried past in a nurse's uniform, a red-haired child on her back, rolling a tractor through her hair.

None of them seemed happy.

After talking with more people, the girls learned it wasn't just toys that were governed by law. Hair colour determined what colour clothes they must wear and what jobs they must do.

People with blonde-hair had to wear red and serve or care for the community; from nurses and doctors to vets and shop-keepers.

Red-headed people must wear pink and work in positions of authority; from policewomen and policemen to teachers and politicians.

Dark-haired people had to wear green and take jobs in the sports or entertainment industry or work at sea or in the air, whilst brown-haired folk had to wear orange and do work that involved making something; be it food, buildings or art.

It was just the way it was: the law of the land. So people accepted it and got on with their lives, miserably.

"We need to do something about this," said Eva.

Maxi and B nodded.

The village was such a beautiful place, with lovely people living in it, yet their talents and dreams were being wasted and they weren't free to do what they wanted.

"These people are trapped," said Eva.

"Laws are meant to protect you, not trap you," said B, whose mum was a policewoman and loved her job.

As the girls turned the corner, the sun went behind a cloud and Maxi removed her cap.

People began to stare.

Maxi began to blush.

"They're looking at your rainbow hair," said B, rubbing her friend's arm softly.

Before long, a small crowd had gathered.

"Hey! Rainbow girl," a little boy piped up. "What toys do you have to play with?"

"There's red in her hair, so she's got a skateboard," said another.

"But, she's got blonde in it too, and it's dark round the back," said a lady.

Maxi smiled.

"My hair is all kinds of colours," she laughed. "And I like all kinds of stuff."

Eva and B held her hand.

The crowd of confused people looked at each other, then back to Maxi.

"All of us are different," said Eva to the crowd. "We're unique. We've different coloured hair, likes and dislikes. We're a whole spectrum of colours, like a rainbow."

"Like Maxi's hair!" smiled B.

The growing crowd smiled back.

"I just want to be as me as I can be," smiled B.

"Me too!" said Maxi.

"The me-est me," giggled Eva.

"I'm the only me there will ever be," Maxi declared.

"So nothing should hold us back from being who we are," said Eva. "And nobody should be told what to wear, play with, or who to be, just because of the colour of their hair."

"How many of you are happy?" asked Eva.

Just two people raised their hands. But nobody else did.

"Wouldn't you all be happier if you were free to be yourselves? To play with the toys you wanted to, wear clothes in the colour of your choice, and work in a job that you've always dreamed of?" asked Maxi. "Because, toys, colours, hobbies and jobs are for everyone."

"Yes!" said a girl. "Me too!" said a boy. "I would!" said a man. "We all would" added a lady.

Before long the crowd chatted away excitedly, imagining what life might be like, if only they had the freedom to choose, if only they were able to be themselves.

So Eva, Maxi and B called a meeting. They invited everyone in the village to attend, even the Mayor.

B told everyone how much she loved football, despite having blonde hair. "One day I hope to play football for a big team, maybe even for my country!" she declared. "Football is my spark."

Maxi explained how much she loved skating, drawing and painting and how her rainbow hair made her feel colourful, like her pictures. "I just want to make things and zoom around," she laughed.

The villagers laughed with her.

Eva talked about her dream to be a scientist and how she loves climbing trees, studying bugs, building dens and observing wildlife with her binoculars.

"We all like climbing trees to be honest," added B, putting her arms around the other girls.

The crowd cheered. Then the girls asked each of them what they loved to do and what they dreamed of becoming?

"What's your spark?" they asked.

The crowd fell silent.

Until one brave blonde haired girl stood up, "I love to dance and sing and I want to be a musician," she said, "I wish I didn't have to be a nurse."

Everybody clapped.

"I'd love to be a nurse, or a vet," said a brown-haired girl, "but I'm not allowed."

A dark-haired boy stood up with his dark-haired dad, "I love to cook and dream of becoming a chef," said the boy. "But I can't." The dad shook his head and placed his hand on his son's shoulder. "I work at sea and fix boats for a living, but I'd much rather fix people who are hurt."

The clapping got louder.

A red-haired man raised his hand, "I've been working as a policeman for years but I really love to make things, I'd much rather be a builder."

"I love playing with diggers and dolls," said a dark haired boy, and my favourite colours are pink and purple. I don't really like green very much, but I'm told I should and must wear it."

Then a little blonde boy stood up, "I love playing with trains and fairies," but I'm not allowed to play with trains. One day I want to be a train-driver."

The cheers rang out across the village hall and down the street towards the city.

"So what are we going to do about it?" asked B.

"Things need to change around here," added Maxi.

"Mayor?" said Eva, inviting the mayor up on stage.

A man with a red moustache and crop of orange hair stood up and joined the girls on stage.

"All my life I've loved the theatre," said the Mayor. "The only thing I like about being mayor is being on stage," he laughed. "All I've ever wanted to do is be an actor!"

The crowd rose from their chairs and clapped, nodding.

"I'll get a message to the Prime Minister right away. These laws of ours need to change."

"There's no need to get a message to me," came a serious voice from the back of the hall.

It was the Prime Minister.

The crowd fell silent.

The PM shook her mop of red curls and strode towards the Mayor and the three girls.

She grabbed the microphone from the Mayor and spoke.

"I've never liked wearing pink and I wake up each morning having dreamt of becoming a pilot" said the Prime Minister.

The crowd went wild.

"I pledge from this day forward that nobody will be told what to wear, what to play with or who to be, based on the colour of their hair. We shall be free to choose and, in doing so, we shall become our very best selves – playing with, wearing and doing what we love."

The next day the village was the cheeriest it had ever been.

Meanwhile, the new Mayor and the new Prime Minister, (who'd been stuck being a Shopkeeper and a Taxi Driver) worked together on a new system to help people become whatever they wanted to be, practice hard and do the jobs they dreamed of doing.

Shop managers tore down the signs and replaced them with shiny new "Toys For All" signage.

Brothers, sisters, cousins and friends swapped toys at a Great Big Toy Swap Shop event the girls organised, and everyone wore all the colours of the rainbow and smiled big happy smiles.

Everyone, that was, except Maxi.

"What's the matter Maxi?" said Eva and B.

"Seeing everyone happy with their families made me think of mine," she sniffed.

"I miss them and I want to go home now."

"Me too," said Eva and B. "But how do we get back?"

A boy in the crowd noticed the girls' worried faces and overheard them.

"Stop!" he called, but nobody heard his gentle voice, so he rang the village bell.

Gradually everyone stopped and listened.

"Our friends have helped change our lives," said the boy. "Now we need to help them get home."

A sporty little blonde-haired girl who'd always wanted a trampoline but had never been allowed one until now, told the girls to meet her at the entrance to the woods.

The whole village came to thank the girls and say goodbye. A gentle dark-haired boy ran over to Eva, Maxi and B, clutching a doll in his hand and gave them a group hug.

"Thank you for standing up for what you believed in," said the Mayor "and for giving us our freedom to choose who to be," added the Prime Minster.

Eva, Maxi and B beamed. But it was time to go home.

"We'll come back and visit," promised B.

"Please do," chorused the new Prime Minister and the old Prime Minister together.

With that, the girls took turns to bounce on the trampoline and 'whooosh', off they flew up into the air, through the invisible door and into their own woodland.

The soft leaves underneath the great oak cushioned their fall.

The three of them leapt up and ran home as fast as their legs could carry them to tell their families all that had happened.

The girls felt so happy to be home and so happy to be free to be themselves.

The next morning, their mums and dads arranged
a shopping trip to reward the girls for being brave
enough to stand up and make a difference.

At the supermarket, the girls ran toward the girls' aisle to find new outfits.

Maxi wanted a top with a skateboard on it, Eva wanted some new climbing boots and a dinosaur coat and B wanted... can you guess what B wanted?

A football kit of course.

The only problem was, they couldn't find any of that in the girls' aisle. A sea of pink princesses, hearts and butterflies was all they could find.

The girls looked at each other, sighed, then grinned.

They knew exactly what they needed to do.

Dear Shop Manager,

We're girls and we like football, dinosaurs, skateboards and climbing trees.

Some of of our friends prefer princesses and butterflies and so does one of our brothers. Another brother loves cars and trains best of all.

That's a lot of different stuff, because we are all different and we all like a big mixture of different things. We don't like things that are labelled as 'boy' things or 'girl' things, we like things that are Eva, Maxi or B things.

What do you like?

Our mummies and daddies told us we are each unique and that, when we grow up, we can be whatever we want to be if we work hard. No limits. This makes us feel happy.

So we felt puzzled, sad and limited when we couldn't find anything we liked in the girls' aisle, because we are girls after all. Girls and boys come in all different shapes and sizes and like all kinds of different things.

We did find some football and skateboarding tops that we LOVED, but they were in the boys' aisle. But, it's not just boys who like sport. It's a bit like saying only people with blonde hair like sport, and that's just silly.

We know you want to make it easy for people to find what they want and you want to sell lots of stuff. We think that might be why you separate clothes in this way. So we've got an idea:

How about putting all the tops together and all the dresses together and all the trousers together? That'd make it even easier for people to shop. You could even get rid of the signs that say 'Boys' and 'Girls'?

We don't think anybody should be told what they should wear, play with or who they should be, based on whether they are a boy or a girl. Because toys, colours and hobbies are for everyone. Thank you for your time and consideration.

Yours sincerely
Eva, Maxi and B (The Climbing Trees Girls)
xoxoxo

Questions for teachers/parents to ask children

Do you think it's ok to tell people, "that's for girls only" or "that's for boys only?" Why/why not?

Why do you think people sometimes do say that, especially shops and adverts?

Do you think there are other ways they could achieve those goals (to sell more/make it easier for shoppers) without grouping clothes/toys as 'for boys/for girls'?

How do you think it might make someone feel if we tell them something they love is for the opposite sex (i.e. for boys only or for girls only?)

Do you think it's important to be yourself and to be proud to be all that you are? Why?

How do you think it would make you feel if you got to focus on your unique strengths?

Did you know before 1890 many baby boys were dressed in pink?

A stereotype is a widely held but fixed and oversimplified image or idea of a particular type of person or thing. Stereotypes can make it easier for us to categorise things and people, but that doesn't make them accurate. This book aims to help children see past stereotypes so they can be themselves and, in doing so, maximise their potential and well-being.

Author's Note

When we tell our children (or other peoples' children) 'that's for boys' or 'that's for girls', it makes about as much sense as saying 'that's for people with blonde hair' or 'that's for people with dark hair'. These stereotypes can stop them from being all that they are. Yet, being ourselves is important to our self-esteem and growth as individuals. As such, nobody should be told what to play with, what to wear or who to be based on their gender, nor based on the colour of their hair, skin or eyes.

Girls and boys are not a different species, we're all part of the same race; the human race and we all have feelings, whatever colour hair, skin, eyes we have and whether we are a boy or a girl.

According to various scientific studies, "our presumed gender differences are really more stereotype than science."[1] So we shouldn't let stereotypes stop us from playing with, wearing or being something that feels right to us, nor should we let stereotypes limit our strengths, abilities or sense of self.

So let's be ourselves and let other people be themselves too. Let's be kind to other people, find our spark and build on our strengths so we can be our happiest best selves, proud to be all that we are, and help other people to do that too.

Thank you for reading this book, which aims to challenge stereotypes and encourage children to be proud to be all that they are. Should you be free to be yourself? If you ask anyone, they'll all agree:

YES YOU CAN!

_____

[1] Parenting Beyond Pink & Blue, Dr Christia Spears Brown

23785049R00030

Printed in Poland
by Amazon Fulfillment
Poland Sp. z o.o., Wrocław